The Day the Trash Came Out to Play

by David M. Beadle   illustrated by Laurie A. Faust

Ezra's Earth Publishing
South Pasadena, CA

Book Design by Kim Grover, Abierto Design
Printed in Singapore by Tien Wah Press
Color Separations by Pace + Navigator

 Printed on Recycled Paper

Publisher's Cataloging-in-Publication
   (Provided by Quality Books, Inc.)

Beadle, David M.
    The day the trash came out to play / by David M.
Beadle, illustrated by Laurie A Faust. -- 1st ed.
    p. cm.
    SUMMARY: Robin's careless disposal of a candy wrapper
creates a litter problem that teaches him about taking
care of his neighborhood.
    Audience: Ages 3-8.
    LCCN 2003094957
    ISBN 0-9727855-0-7

    1. Litter (Trash)--Juvenile fiction.
2. Environmental protection--Citizen participation--
Juvenile fiction. [1. Litter (Trash)--Fiction.
2. Environmental protection--Fiction.]   I. Faust, Laurie
A. II. Title.

PZ8.3.B3714Da 2004   [E]
                    QBI03-700462

Ezra's Earth is committed to preserving ancient forests and natural resources. We have elected to print this title on Leykam Recycled Matt Art Paper, which is 50% recycled (15% post-consumer and 35% pre-consumer) and processed chlorine free. As a result of our paper choice, Ezra's Earth Publishing has saved the following natural resources:

3.6 trees (40 feet in height)
1050 gallons water
615 kWh electricity
9 pounds of air pollution

We are a member of Green Press Initiative.
For more information about Green Press Initiative visit www.greenpressinitiative.org.

green press INITIATIVE

"We all have to do our part to protect the environment. If we clean up after ourselves, we'll keep our parks, neighborhoods and other special places beautiful so that everyone can enjoy the outdoors."

—Sierra Club

For Debra, who made it all possible. To Evelyn and Jonah, my trash monitors. To Neil and to all little litter conscious citizens everywhere.

—D. M. B.

For Kiersten, Nick, Katie and Emily (my rainbow, sun, stars and moon) and Jeff, my universe.

- L. A. F.

There is a town called Sutton Nash,

a wonderful place to stay.

Except for one time, not long ago,

the day the trash came out to play.

Sutton Nash was neat and tidy
with the cleanest streets of all...
Each leaf was raked, each speck removed
as soon as it would fall.

But then one cool and windy day
a boy walked down the street.
His name was Robin and in his hand,
a delicious, mouth-watering treat.

Robin peeled the pretty paper
that covered up the candy.
He tossed the wrapper on the street—
now it didn't look so dandy.

For at that moment something happened
as quick as fire and a flash—
When the paper hit the ground,
it became a piece of trash.

Robin laughed to see the wind
blow the trash up in the air.
"Soon," he said, "it will blow out of sight,
so I really needn't care."

What Robin forgot to think about, is that it has to go somewhere.

"Help, Help!" cried the little piece of trash.

"I don't want to be blowing free."

And just as it was shouting this,

it hit a bumblebee.

"I beg your pardon," said the wrapper,
"for getting in your way.
But I'm at the whimsy of the wind,
and the wind blows hard today."

Before the wrapper could say farewell,

another gust came down.

It grabbed that worn old piece of paper

and blew it all over town.

Suddenly from every garbage can
other trash came out to play.
Because they saw someone else go first,
they thought it was okay.

Old newspapers, soda cans, egg cartons and lint,

chip packets, broken tennis rackets, old springs and splints,

bottles, a television and a smelly old shoe

(with a hole in the sole where water gets through).

Broken toys and junk mail

(you can be sure there was plenty of that).

There was even a pair of worn out gloves

and a matching scruffy hat.

A couple of kids saw what was happening; they couldn't believe their eyes.

"Look over there!" they shouted out
to the people passing by.

Robin's head got rather dizzy
from all the blowing trash.
He stood there in the dirty street
of filthy Sutton Nash.

Someone asked, "How do we clean up
in this cold and gusty weather?"
Robin spoke up, he had made a plan,
"We must work together!"

When everyone heard what Robin said
they knew what had to be done.
They gathered up the runaway trash:
each piece, one by one.

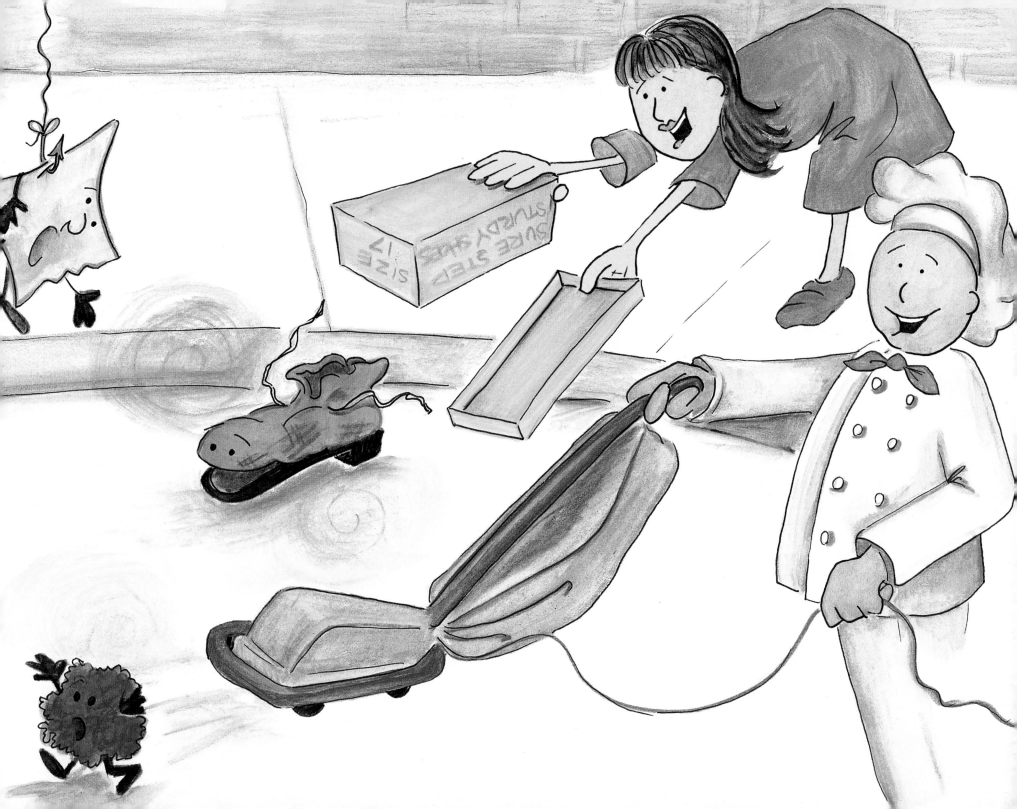

Then they turned to Robin's wrapper
that was blowing in the sky.
They stood upon each other's shoulders,
but still it blew too high.

Then Robin used a fishing net
he borrowed from a boy.
He caught that tired piece of paper,
and everyone cheered with joy.

He threw the paper in the trash
for all the town to see.
"Thank goodness!"
said the candy wrapper.
"This is where I want to be."

A good thing came
from that windy day
when the trash went on a caper.
The town built
a recycling center
for bottles, cans, and paper.

There is a town called Sutton Nash,
a wonderful place to stay.
Except for one time, not long ago,
the day the trash came out to play.

Sutton Nash Times

Where Every Day Is Earth Day

Teaching about litter is not a lot of rubbish

One person discarding a single piece of trash onto the street may not seem like a big deal, but multiply that by many people and litter quickly builds up. Blown around by traffic and wind, trash collects in our street gutters promoting others to litter. Not only does trash make the street look unsightly, it can be a health hazard to people, plants and wildlife.

Public trash cans are another source of litter. On busy days and holidays, these cans fill quickly and overflow. It is always best to take your trash home and dispose of it there. Keeping the lid on your garbage cans at home can also help prevent your household trash from adding to the litter problem.

The four "R's" for minimizing litter are Rethink, Reduce, Reuse, Recycle. **Rethink** what you purchase, the waste it might create and the resources that are used to make and package it. **Reduce** your usage of packaged goods and try to buy in bulk. **Reuse** packaging materials such as water bottles, boxes, shopping bags and packing peanuts. **Recycle** as much as possible by taking plastic containers, glass, cans and paper goods to a recycling center or placing it in the proper containers for street collection. If you have the space, compost food scraps in your yard. This creates an excellent all-natural fertilizer for your flowers and outdoor plants. When you do these four small things - **rethink, reduce, reuse, recycle** - you will be surprised at how little trash you will have left for the garbage collectors.

"Keeping trash off our streets, backyards, and parks protects our ocean, its inhabitants, and ecosystems and creates a healthy future for us all."
-Aquarium of the Pacific, Long Beach, California.

"Our parks have given generations of visitors recreation, adventure, renewal and inspiration, but they need our help. It costs $2.4 million annually for trash removal in California's state parks alone. By packing out trash we can save those precious dollars for ensuring the long-term health of our parks."
-California State Parks Foundation